30119 026 159 06 3

MCL

D0245911

Jodie
Beans

For Liz, with all my love
M.J.D.

With thanks to Walker Books
J.A.

LONDON BOROUGH OF SUTTON LIBRARY SERVICE	
30119 026 159 06 3	
Askews	Dec-2010
JF	

First published 1999 by Walker Books Ltd
87 Vauxhall Walk, London SE11 5HJ

This edition published 2010

2 4 6 8 10 9 7 5 3 1

Text © 1999 Malachy Doyle
Illustrations © 1999 Judith Allibone

The moral rights of the author and illustrator
have been asserted

This book has been typeset in Usherwood

Printed in China

All rights reserved. No part of this book may be
reproduced, transmitted or stored in an information
retrieval system in any form or by any means, graphic,
electronic or mechanical, including photocopying,
taping and recording, without prior written permission
from the publisher.

British Library Cataloguing in Publication Data:
A catalogue record for this book is available from the British Library

ISBN 978-1-4063-1861-6

www.walker.co.uk

Jody's Beans

Malachy Doyle

illustrated by Judith Allibone

WALKER BOOKS
AND SUBSIDIARIES
LONDON · BOSTON · SYDNEY · AUCKLAND

It was springtime, and Jody's Granda
came to visit.

He brought Jody a packet of runner beans.

They counted them out on the kitchen table.

"… nine, ten, eleven, twelve," said Granda. "That's enough."

They went out into the garden and found
the sunniest spot where the wind never blew.

They dug the soil and pulled out
all the weeds,

mixed in some compost and raked it over.
Then Jody made twelve holes in a circle,

and put one seed in each.

"Don't forget to water them,
Jody," said Granda.

"What do runner beans look like,
Granda?" asked Jody.

"Wait and see," said Granda.
"Wait and see."

Soon the tiny green plants
pushed their way up through
the dark brown soil.

Jody watered them
every day, unless it rained,
just as she'd been told.

One day the phone rang.
It was Granda.
"Hello, Jody," he said.
"How are the beans?"

"They're growing fast," said Jody.
"Good," said Granda.
"Now listen closely. This is
what I want you to do…"

Jody went down to her vegetable
patch and pulled out the
 smallest plants. Now the
strongest ones had
plenty of room
to grow.

Soon they were as
tall as the cat.

When Granda came to visit again,
he pushed six long canes in the ground
beside the plants, and tied them
together at the top.

He looped string round and
round the poles, all the way
up from the bottom.

"It's like a
wigwam,"
said Jody.

The next few weeks were hot.
The sun burned down on the garden.

Jody watered her plants
every day.

They snaked up
the wigwam,

hooking themselves on to
the string as they went.

"Granda," she said on the phone,
"they're bigger than me now!"
"That's great, Jody," said Granda.

"How big will they get?" Jody asked.

"Wait and see," said Granda.

"Wait and see."

Then the rain came.
Lots and lots of it.
Jody hardly had to
water the plants at all.

They grew bigger
every day, and bright
red flowers burst out
all over them.

"They're so beautiful,
Dad," said Jody.

After the warm
sunny days
returned the
first beans
appeared.

The plants reached the
top of the poles,
and Granda
came to
visit again.

"They're even
taller than you,
Granda!" said Jody.

"They're wonderful beans, Jody," Granda
said, pinching the tips at the tops of the
poles. "You must have green fingers, just
like your Granda."

"Will the baby have green fingers
too, Granda?" asked Jody.

"Wait and see,"
said Granda.
"Wait and see."

"It's time to find out
what they taste like,"
said Granda.

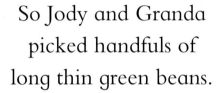

"Oh," said Jody, "I didn't
know we were going
to eat them!"

So Jody and Granda
picked handfuls of
long thin green beans.

They topped
and tailed them,

sliced and boiled them,

and served them up
with butter.

"Mmm!" said Mum. "They're delicious."

27

The beans grew on and on,
right into the autumn.

Jody picked them
every day.

If she missed one, it grew hard and
knobbly. Mum had to cut the stringy
edges off. It didn't taste as nice.

At the end of autumn Granda and Jody
picked the very last beans.

They were the ones right up
at the top of the poles where
Jody couldn't reach.

They were gigantic!

"They're no good,"
said Jody sadly.

"Oh yes they are,"
said Granda.

And he opened
them up, took out
the seeds, and spread
the twelve biggest ones
in a circle on the
kitchen table.

"Do you know what these
are for, Jody?" he asked.
"Yes, Granda," said Jody, smiling.
"They're next year's runner beans!"

"And how tall do you
think they'll grow?"
asked Granda.

"Wait and see,
Granda," said Jody.
"Wait and see."

Index

About the Author

Malachy Doyle lives on a little island
off the north west coast of Ireland.
His favourite sight in the garden is
the runner beans in full flower –
a mass of bright scarlet, with the
prospect of tasty meals to come.
He recommends frying the smallest,
tenderest beans you can find in
butter and garlic – delicious!